About the Book

The day the new refrigerator arrived in its large brown carton, Christina Katerina and her mother were both excited—but for very different reasons.

"Oh, how grand and new!" said Christina's mother, looking at the refrigerator. "It is! Oh, it really is!" murmured Christina, looking at the box, which she immediately dragged to the front yard.

In a series of hilarious episodes, the box becomes a castle, a clubhouse, and other imaginations in which Christina and her friend Fats swear undying friendship, wage furious battles, and drive Christina's mother crazy.

In this lively story, Patricia Gauch has caught the wonderful ability of boys and girls to use their imaginations with the most common object. Doris Burn, well-known illustrator of *Andrew Henry's Meadow*, shows each transformation of the box in all its glorious detail.

CHRISTINA KATERINA

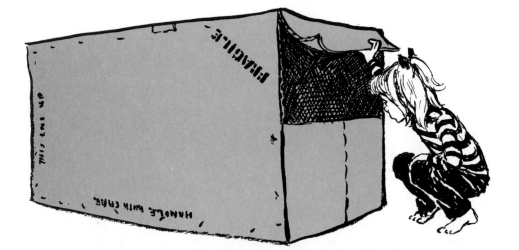

& THE BOX

by Patricia Lee Gauch

Illustrated by Doris Burn

PAPERSTAR

The Putnam & Grosset Group

Weekly Reader is a registered trademark of Weekly Reader Corporation.

2002 Edition

Printed on recycled paper

Printed in the United States of America
L. C. number: 71-133926
ISBN 0-698-11676-3

For our Christina

Christina Katerina liked *things*:
tin cups and old dresses,
worn-out ties and empty boxes.
Any of those things, but mostly boxes.
Hat boxes,
bakery boxes with see-through lids,
shoe boxes.

Best of all she liked big boxes. So she was happy in-deed one sleepy summer day — when even her some-times-friend Fats Watson was out of town — to see a truck deliver a great, tall box. It came on a refrigerator.

"Oh, how grand and new," Christina's mother said, looking at the refrigerator.

"It is! Oh, it really is!" said Christina, looking at the box.

And she quickly claimed the box for her own and dragged it under the apple tree.

To Mother, who was very neat and tidy, it seemed that boxes were for basements or trash barrels, not for front yards under the apple tree. But she decided that it couldn't hurt — it couldn't possibly hurt — for one day or two to have the big box in the front yard, there under the apple tree.

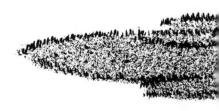

That afternoon Christina's father cut a window and door in the box, and Christina painted on turrets, a drawbridge, and bolts for the door. And the box became...a castle. Inside, she put sticks on the window for iron bars, and she brought in all her cups and saucers and a lot of Fig Newtons in case there was a battle and she couldn't get out.

FRAGILE

For two days she and her bears lived and played in her castle peacefully.

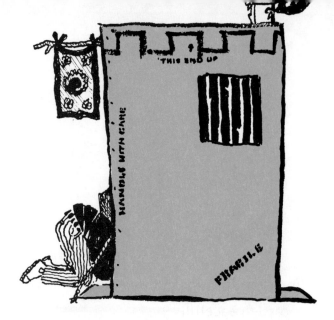

Until Fats Watson came home. He sneaked into her castle while she was out to lunch and ate all her Fig Newtons, and she locked him in until he hollered, "I'm sorry," fifteen times.

When she finally let him out, Fats gave Christina's castle a kick and over it went, smack, on its side.

Mother came out and saw the fallen box. "I see that's
the end of the castle, Christina," she said with a smile
and started to haul it away.

"But that's no castle," said Christina, hauling it back
again. "That's my clubhouse!"

And it was...for three long days. Right there under the apple tree.

Christina changed the window into a door and the door into a window. She put in two benches for members and a chair for the president, and she painted "Keep out," "Members only," and "Danger to enemies" on the outside.

And she let Fats join. Then they met in the club-house (which was very dark when the door was closed and very secret), and they spit on a nickel and swore to be friends forever.

And they were.

Until one day when Fats got angry at always being vice-president. He climbed on the clubhouse roof and promised to sit there until Christina made him president.

Only the roof caved in first, and Christina disbanded
the club.

When Mother saw the sat-in box, she brushed her hands together. Now she would have her nice neat yard. "Well," she said. "*That* is the end of the club-house!" and she tugged it toward the street.

"But that's no clubhouse," said Christina, tugging it back again. "That's my racing car, Hermione, and I'm late for a race."

Before speeding off, Christina put the top on the bottom, turned the window into a cockpit, and on the sides painted two magnificent curling silver horns which she blasted at Fats every time she rounded the apple tree.

For two days she raced around the yard and won every time.

Until Fats said he'd take a look at the motor, that
it didn't sound quite right.

When he cut off the nose to get at the motor, the car collapsed.

Christina's mother was relieved. "Well, that *is* the end of the racing car," she said, and she pulled the cardboard toward the trash barrel.

"But that's no racing car," said Christina, pulling it back again. "That's the floor of my summer mansion, and I'm going to have a ball!"

And she did. Right there under the apple tree.

She patted the box out flat and drew furniture on each flap. A stove and refrigerator for the kitchen, a bed for the bedroom, and a grand piano and a violin for the living room so there would be music for her ball.

Then she and her bears and Fats dressed up in gowns
and high heels, and they invited kings and queens and
some presidents and one vice-president to come. And
everybody came, and they danced and danced until
their feet hurt and they had to take off their shoes.
Even without shoes Christina had a wonderful time.

Until Fats decided the floor needed scrubbing. He sprayed it down with the garden hose and mopped it

until the floor puckered and grew lumpy and finally
fell apart.

When Mother came out a little later and looked at
her front yard, she shook her head and said, "Well!"
And then: "Is this the end of your grand floor?"

"What floor?" asked Christina, who was running by.
"Oh, you mean that old ragged box? Let's do throw
it away."

Mother breathed a sigh. At last she could have her nice neat yard.

"But quick!" Christina said....

"Fat's mother got a washer and drier today, and he's bringing two ships down now. I said my mother wouldn't mind a bit if we sailed them here in our front yard...right under our apple tree."

About the Author

Patricia Lee Gauch grew up in Detroit, Michigan. While living in Westchester County, she was a member of the Jean Fritz Writer's Workshop. She now lives in Hyde Park, New York, spending summers in an old red farmhouse near Lexington, Michigan.

About the Artist

Since she was nine years old and first set foot on a small island in Puget Sound, Washington, Doris Burn wanted to live on an island. Her wish came true and for a number of years she lived on Waldron in Puget Sound, which looks out on the channel and the beautiful Canadian islands.

Originally, Mrs. Burn lived in Portland, Oregon, where she was born. She attended the universities of Oregon, Hawaii and Washington. Today she makes her home in Bellingham, Washington.

Doris Burn is the author-illustrator of *Andrew Henry's Meadow*, *The Summerfolk*, and the illustrator of *Hudden and Dudden and Donald O'Neary*, an old Celtic folktale adapted by Joseph Jacobs, *We Were Tired of Living in a House* by Liesel Moak Skorpen and *My Old Tree* by Patricia Lee Gauch.